This book belongs to

....

Me!

HODDER CHILDREN'S BOOKS

First published in Great Britain in 2017 by Hodder and Stoughton.

Text © Alison Steadman 2017

Illustrations © Mark Chambers 2017

The moral rights of the author and illustrator have been asserted.

PB ISBN: 978 1 444 93350 5

HB ISBN: 978 1 444 93349 9

10 9 8 7 6 5 4 3 2 1

Printed and bound in China.

Hodder Children's Books An imprint of Hachette Children's Group Part of Hodder and Stoughton

Carmelite House 50 Victoria Embankment London EC4Y0DZ

An Hachette UK Company www.hachette.co.uk

www.hachettechildrens.co.uk

A CIP catalogue record of this book is available from the British Library.

MIX
Paper from responsible sources
FSC® C104740
www.fsc.org

For Jess, who always rescues
the spiders in our house!

– M.C.

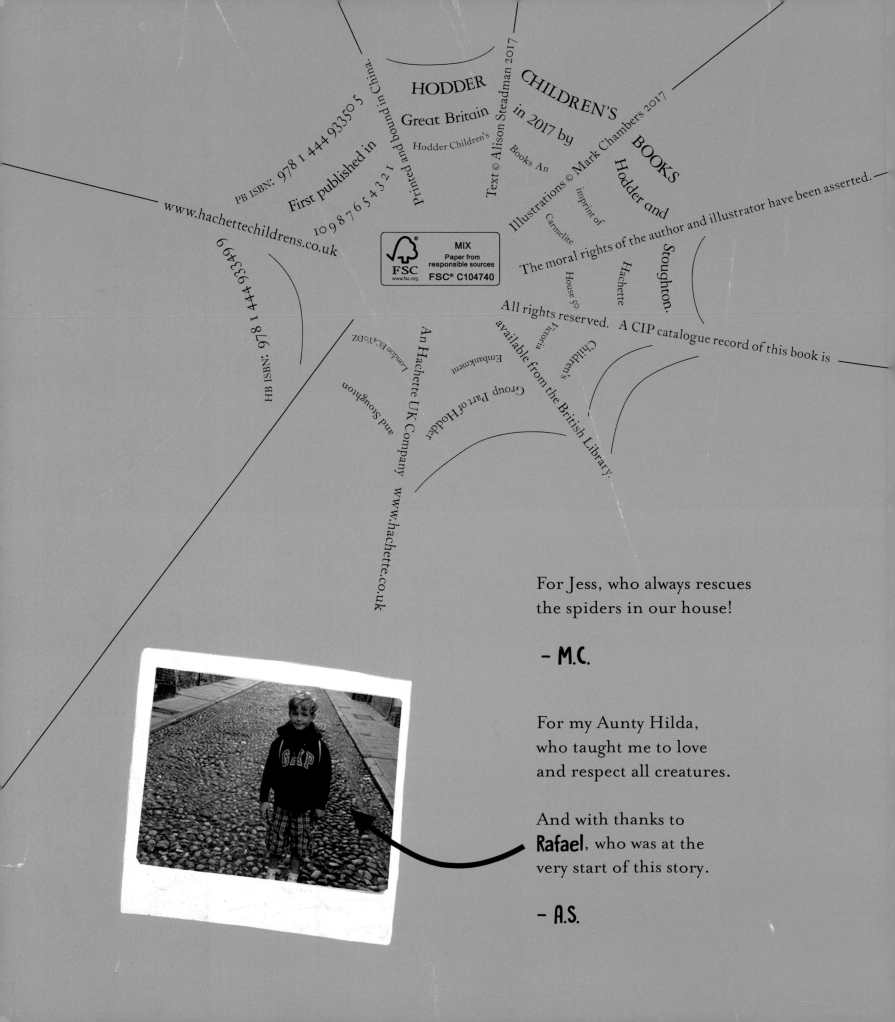

For my Aunty Hilda,
who taught me to love
and respect all creatures.

And with thanks to
Rafael, who was at the
very start of this story.

– A.S.

ALISON STEADMAN

SPIDER!

ILLUSTRATED BY
MARK CHAMBERS

Hodder
Children's
Books

It was another ordinary afternoon
in Rafael's house, until ...

FACT!

Spiders' legs are great
— they can even run
upside down on the ceiling!

Dad swished and swatted, but he just couldn't catch the spider.

I hate spiders!

FACT!

Spiders are great at jumping. They use spider silk as a safety rope!

Later, Rafael was in the bathroom.
He was humming happily to himself
as he brushed his teeth, until...

Rafael and Chips couldn't believe it.

Er... did you just SPEAK?

I can't get out of the bath! It's too slippy. Can you help? I don't wear shoes like you!

FACT!

Some spiders can't climb out of slippy baths. All they need is something they can use as a ladder! Try a towel – or your arm!

Rafael threw a towel over the edge of the bath, keeping as FAR AWAY as possible from the **BIG HAIRY SCARY SPIDER!**

What if it **BITES?**

FACT!
House spiders don't bite people! In fact, spiders don't even have the ability to chew.

The next morning… Rafael opened his eyes and the **BIG HAIRY SCARY SPIDER** was still there!

Thank you for rescuing me last night! Are we friends now?

FACT!

Spiders have 48 knees!
Six per leg, for eight legs …
makes 48!

I'm not sure I want to be your friend! You've got long hairy scary legs!

Oh, that's nothing! I'll show you some legs that are EVEN HAIRIER!

What's wrong with hairy legs?

Rafael gulped. And followed the spider.

FACT!

All spiders are hairy – just like all humans! Spiders use the hairs to work out where they are, to smell and taste, and even to attract other spiders.

FACT!

Engineers are studying spider silk to work out how spiders can make it so strong. Maybe one day it might be used to build aeroplanes!

Rafael thought the web was amazing.

Wowsy! You're like a **superhero!**

SPINNERET – for making super-strong silk.

FACT!

Spiders LOVE eating flies! Some spiders eat as many as two thousand flies and other insects each year.

HOUSE SPIDERS: FAVOURITE FOODS

Anything they can catch!

MENU

1. Flies
2. Moths
3. Cockroaches
4. Bedbugs
5. Crickets

FACT!

Did you know that spiders
are found all over the world?
On every continent except Antarctica!

Suddenly, the door opened . . .

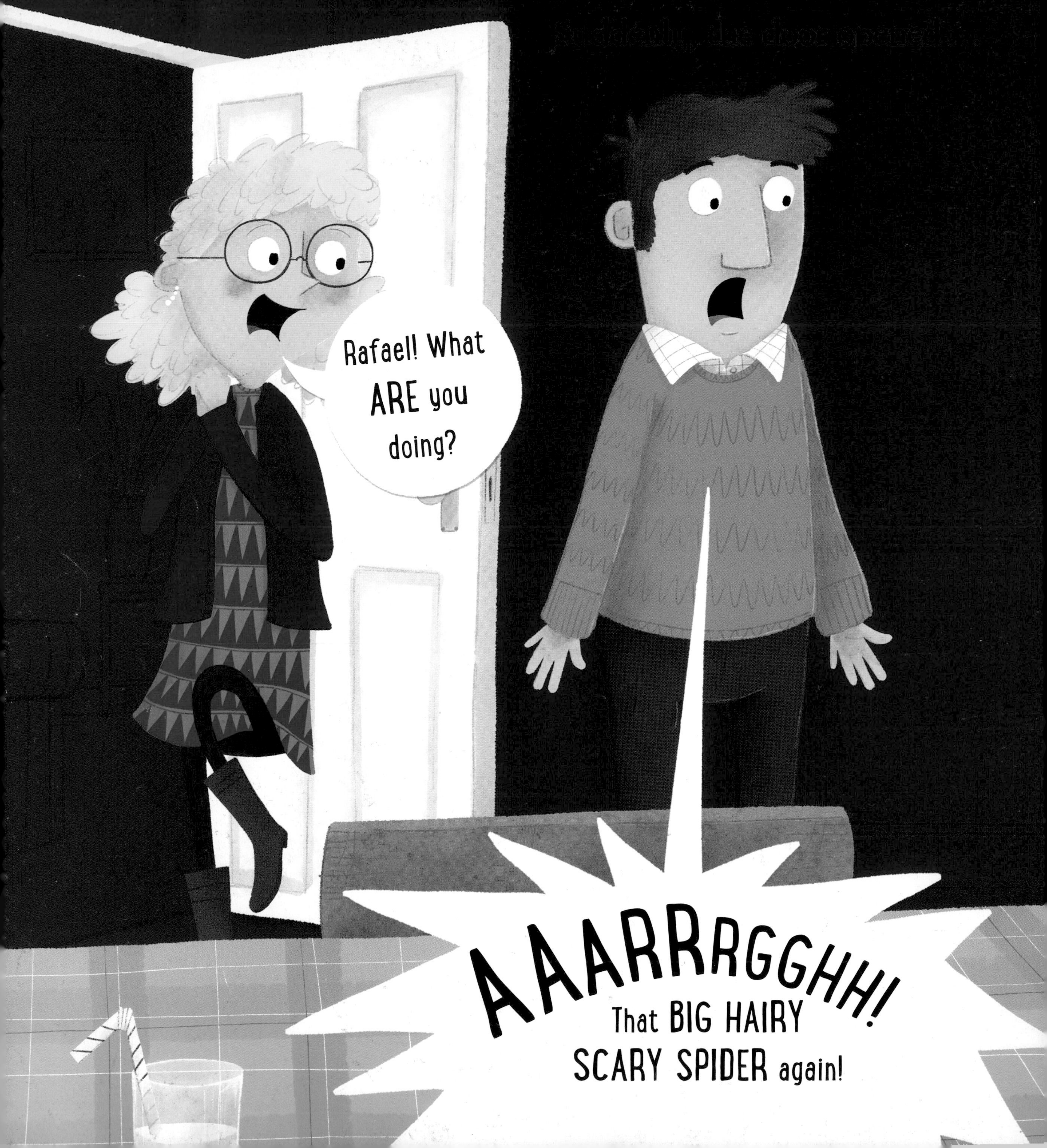

And so Spidy kept teaching Rafael, and they became the BEST of friends...

You can take off your coat. And I can shed my exoskeleton! Look! Ex-o-skel-e-ton!

FACT!

Spiders can shed their coats — their exoskeletons — eight times before they become adults.

MY HOUSE SPIDER PLEDGE

1. I will never squash a spider.

2. I will always help spiders out of the bath.

3. I will remember that spiders have feelings too!

Signed: ....